Jamie

Sam And The Magic Tree

Rachel Bolton

BALBOA.PRESS
A DIVISION OF HAY HOUSE

Balboa Press books may be ordered through booksellers or by contacting:

Balboa Press
A Division of Hay House
1663 Liberty Drive
Bloomington, IN 47403
www.balboapress.co.uk
UK TFN: 0800 0148647 (Toll Free inside the UK)
UK Local: 02036 956325 (+44 20 3695 6325 from outside the UK)

Print information available on the last page.

ISBN: 978-1-9822-8153-3 (sc)
ISBN: 978-1-9822-8154-0 (e)

Balboa Press rev. date: 07/09/2020

For Sam and Mother Earth

CHAPTER ONE

Welcome to the magical land of Amazonia on the planet of Mystery. Amazonia is blessed with exquisite flowers and trees that shine with beautiful iridescent colours. There are abundant fruits and wild foods that benefit from the nurture and quality of the land. The crystal clear rivers and lakes are full of magic and wonder and enjoyed by all who meet with them. The air is sweet and clear to breathe, carrying with it all the fragrances of the sun-kissed land and the sky, a tapestry of colour that continuously changes throughout the day.

My name is Sam, and I am an Amazonian. I have a story to tell and invite you to join me on a journey, from when I was ten years old.

Amazonia is home for many, including the Amazonians. They are about one and a half metres high and have large flat feet and knobbly knees. The trunk of their body is quite long and so are their arms - always helpful when picking fruit from the trees. Their hair can be dark brown or blonde and is usually quite curly. Their faces are long, with the females having emerald green eyes and the males brown eyes. The folk work hard but in a balanced way, ensuring that their families are provided for as well as expressing all their divine creativity. All the Amazonians respect themselves and others and everyone's creative side is acknowledged and nurtured, especially in their younger years.

"Come on Kit we have to get home for dinner!"

We both ran home and I fell against the door puffing as I bent over double. I had a stitch and Kit just met my head as it came down to his eye level and he gave me a big sloshy kiss.

"Yuck-thanks, Kit-Just what I needed!"

"Hello Mother, I'm home!"

"Hello Sam, how was your day?"

"It was good! Oh, the fire is wonderful, and the food smells great. Is it nearly ready?"

"Yes it is, so go wash your hands and come sit down my hungry, Sam!"

My Mother had brought me up by herself in our cosy wooden house tucked beneath a beautiful Freeland tree, near enough to a small stream that we could hear her musical flow when our doors and windows were open.

"How was your day?" I asked.

"It was fine, I had two animals for healing with sore feet. They are fine now, and hopefully, they will be skipping the whole way home."

My Mother is gifted as a healer and can channel high vibrational energy that can heal the sick. She works with all the folk from Amazonia who come from all over the kingdom to receive her help.

"What else did you do?"

"Oh yes, I also spent some time by the river which was a real gift as I fell asleep and had an amazing dream of little people beneath the Earth!"

"Really! How strange, what do you think it means?"

"I don't know at the moment, but I am sure it will all reveal itself very soon!"

"It's best we get an early night tonight Sam we have a busy day tomorrow; we are going on a trek! I have to collect herbs from the edge of the forest, and I want you to meet someone very special to me."

"Who is that?" I asked with my face rolling up in its inquisitive way.

Mother gave me a magical smile with a twinkle in her eyes. "You will see it is a surprise!"

"Oh, please, tell me now!" I said, bending over sideways on the chair.

"Well, think on this. He has four legs and is magical, and I have known him for a long, long time." She replied with another glint in her eye.

"Oooh, who is that then? And why have I not heard of him before?" I asked as I tried hard to work out who it could be.

"Ok Sam, come on it is time to go to bed, the morning will reveal all to you."

I hugged her goodnight and walked into the cosiness of my bedroom. The firelight caught the room with its warm glow as its colours painted the interior with its loving presence and Kit was laying by the fire. Because of my gift of hearing the thoughts of animals, I had an inner knowing about Kit's thoughts. Kit rolled over onto his side and let out a huge sigh. He knew that he had a long walk ahead of him in the morning and was already a little tired from the adventure of today. He too was thinking about who this mystery being could be.

I woke up the next morning, smiled and stretched my body until it felt like my elastic band limbs could take no more. I coiled my self back into a curled up position, snug in my blue and white striped pyjamas.

Kit launched himself up on to my bed and encouraged me to get up. "Come on Sam, it's time to go. Rachel has already packed her basket and is waiting for you."

"Alright, Kit. I hear you."

I quickly put on my long trousers of thick green material and tied the rope around my waist. I pulled on a fresh green shirt that smelt of the flowers Mother had lovingly washed it in. Once I had retrieved two socks from under my bed, I opened my bedroom door and met Mother sitting at the table by the fireplace.

"Good morning Sam, would you like some breakfast before we go, or will you eat a little along the way?"

"Oh along the way, I am most excited for the day."

We stepped out of the house and walked down to the river to a place where we had made a stone footbridge that helped us cross over to the other side. The river was calm, and the sunlight was dancing upon it like stars that had been left from the night before.

We both acknowledged the river, said good morning and wished her a joyful day and continued out into the fields in the direction of the forest.

"What's that sound?" I asked.

"I am not sure, but I have a feeling we should turn back home."

One of the most important things my Mother had taught me over my few years was to always discern my feelings and then act upon my inner knowing. So with no more said, we just turned around and headed home.

CHAPTER TWO

The Amazonians did not realise that anything other than rock and earth was below their feet. However, underneath the surface lives the kingdom of the dwarves. The dwarves are about sixty centimetres tall and very strong. The males have large, thick forearms and hands that are as strong as strong can be. Their legs are muscular and powerful, and always seem to be slightly bent at the knees. Their large feet with five toes are broad, which enables them to be in good contact with the land and her energies, which is a good thing, as they draw much of their nutrition from the energy of the earth. The dwarves work hard every day, and so the muscles around their tummies and backs are sturdy as well. They live a very long time, on average about two hundred years, and even when they grow older, they are still as strong as they were in their youth. The longer the Soul of a dwarf lives within their physical body, the more wisdom they gain; but a dwarf's body is not programmed by any belief that it has to age and decay. This means the dwarves are happy, healthy, and express their divine qualities up until it is time for them to pass on to another life.

The females are the same height as the males but not as thick muscled. The female dwarfs are amazing artists and create every day. They use natural pigments from the land to paint on the walls of some of the caves and love to create works of art using the natural clays within the earth. They also produce all the cups, plates and bowls that are required but they do not stop there. They create magical art. Clay sculptures are made, and then life is breathed into them during spiritual ceremonies. The female dwarfs will sit in a circle, singing and chanting ancient songs and then they use their breath to carry the magic into the completed sculptures. Once alive, they become toy friends for the younger dwarves. The lifespan of one of these enchanted sculptures can vary, but usually it is only from a few days to a few weeks. This is accepted by the younger dwarves and the sculptures themselves. This allows for a natural cycle of life and death to happen just like it does with the seasons within, upon and above the planet. The female dwarfs are responsible for bearing and raising children. They pass on their knowledge and the wisdom of where they have come from and what it is they are here to do. They meditate in groups daily to hold the magical space within the caves. They are also wonderful cooks and use all the natural resources to feed everyone. They require some food, but much of the energy they require is absorbed through the souls of their feet and their higher self! They know that only a small aspect of themselves is within their physical body and so they consciously tune into their higher spirit which in turn gives them more energy for life.

Some of the tunnels and caves can be miles beneath the surface as well as just below it. The dwarves are custodians of their home and responsible for maintaining the beautiful, magical spaces within the crystal-filled caves that are a stunning sight to see. Clear and colourful crystals grow on the ground and from the roof of the caves. Some are as tall as the caves themselves and others are smaller but just as powerful. The crystals emit a bright, magical glow and have a presence and power that is immeasurable. The energy that feeds these wise crystals come from many sources including, the planet's earth spirits and elementals as well as the ones who live on the surface. When all the folk are happy and loving to themselves and others, they generate some of the energy required by the crystals in the caves to glow. This is because within the heart centre of each and everyone, there is a beautiful power source that is immense and when everyone's energy is combined, it is magnificent. This energy force is completely unseen by most individuals, but felt by the body of the planet. The beautiful combination of energy from the nature spirits, the land herself, the Amazonians, the animals, the insects, and even the weather, all feed the planet with love and energy, allowing all the trees, flowers, crops and everything alive to grow strong and healthily. The energy also resonates within the water, creating beautiful crystal clear, healing, serene waterways. This is a natural part of the cycle of life that is so important to Amazonia and the rest of the planet of Mystery, including the ones who rely on their environment for food and water to live healthy lives.

It is the job of the male dwarves to maintain the crystal caves. Sometimes the earth shifts, displacing lots of rock and earth that will need to be moved. Once everything is cleared all the crystals are inspected to ensure all is well with them. Sometimes the caves collapse onto the dwarfs while they are working, but as you already know, they are very, very strong and so they just cover their heads, bend forward a little and let the earth fall. They understand that the planet does not want to hurt them, so they trust the whole process and wait until the tremors, the shifting and the shaking of the earth have stopped, and then they go about restoring their caves and tunnels.

CHAPTER THREE

One day, far away from any of the general day-to-day life of the Amazonians, an ancient, sacred stone circle lit up and generated an energy field that made a loud, strange, buzzing sound. All of a sudden, a star-gate manifested surrounded by light. It was a star-gate that had not been seen or used for thousands of years. The gate allowed multidimensional travel for those wanting to move between planets and dimensions from all over the universes. A long succession of a race unknown to the Amazonians, known as the Mopheads appeared. One by one, a thousand soldiers walked through the gate wearing plated armour. Their faces were grey and fierce, and they stomped their feet as they clonked along. They held large pole like weapons that glowed silver in the light, wrapped with a dark metal that spiralled around the top. Once all the soldiers were through they drew to a halt and then the King appeared, a small, gaunt man who looked just as grey as the soldiers.

"Hail King Atmat!" The chief soldier called.

"Hail King Atmat!" The whole army responded.

"Sire, in the name of King Atmat, we claim this kingdom for you!" boomed the chief.

"Very well, let us find somewhere to build my castle!" Said the King in his small squeaky voice.

Just then the Queen came through. She was small and wore a long ivory dress with sequins that made her look luminescent in the sun. Her long blonde hair was gathered into a plait that laid along her back. She too was very grey, but still seemed to hold on to a little sparkle in her blue eyes.

"Hail Queen Sazander!" The chief called out.

"Hail Queen Sazander!" The army replied.

The Royal children then followed though the star-gate.

"Hail Corba, son of King Atmat!" the chief called out.

"Hail Corba!"

The boy just looked on. He was not as strong-looking as the soldiers, but weaker in nature, just like his father, his mother and his sister. The young girl stepped forward and again the chief called out:

"Hail Ria, daughter of King Atmat!"

"Thank you, thank you very much!" replied Ria in a small friendly voice.

"Silence! Have you learnt nothing!" Said the King.

Ria just raised her eyes and continued to survey her new surroundings with her long red hair blowing in the wind. She wore a long green dress that reached down to her ankles, with long pointy green shoes peeking out from beneath. She pulled her purple shawl up around her shoulders as the fresh air bit at her neck and her arms and walked to be closer to her brother. He was standing still, looking perplexed. He wore dark brown trousers and a thick jacket with pockets and a hood that laid down his back. He too felt the fresh air around him and pulled his hood up and gathered his jacket closer to himself to compensate for the feeling of unease.

Corba gave Ria a half-hearted reassuring glance. He wished he could tell her that everything was going to be okay, but he was not sure he believed that himself. He had no idea what his Father's plans were for them and everyone else. They were young adults now but they were still were very connected to their Mother and Corba looked to her for reassurance.

"Where are we Mother?"

"Do not worry my children, your Father has a plan, and we should trust in that alone."

The star-gate was still open and thousands of the King's folk came through.

Scared and raggedy families, each carrying just one bag looked on to their new surroundings. The soldiers rounded them up into a line.

"Let us move forwards, and onwards!" King Atman said to his first chief with minimal regard for the concerns of his family.

The soldiers addressed the people in an authoritative tone:

"Everyone is to walk and follow us, we are in search of a place to build King Atmat his castle, barracks for the army and homes for us all!"

The Royal family were carried by horses adorned with beautiful golden and purple silks. The army marched in lines of four and the King's people followed behind and the soldiers ensured they kept up to speed.

The star-gate closed behind them and the stones were allowed to return to their quiet life nestled within the grass surrounded by beautiful meadow flowers blowing in the breeze. They stood in their circle listening to the soldiers march off in the distance. All twelve stones were very concerned for what had occurred and decided to meld their energies together and send a telepathic message to someone they knew who should be informed of the new arrivals to the planet.

CHAPTER FOUR

The King's army was divided into sections, each with a leader, who answered to the head trooper who was in charge of the whole army and he, in turn, took his orders from the King. Each section contained one hundred male soldiers. Females were not enlisted as soldiers, instead they were utilised as sword, axe and armour makers, cooks and nurses.

Section ten was run by a Mophead called Seltrecmore. A leader now, but he had been a soldier for many years. Seltrecmore was inside his tent talking with some of his men when a messenger arrived and requested that he meet with the head trooper immediately. Seltrecmore, like all the other leaders had been instrumental in the surrender of the Amazonians to the new King and his rule. It had not been that difficult as the Amazonians were a peaceful folk, but the Mopheads had still used a heavy hand to ensure that their rule was taken seriously. Seltrecmore grabbed his sword and walked to the head troopers tent. His name was Shampin, and he was a mighty warrior.

"Sir, you summoned me," said Selctrecmore.

"Indeed I did!" Said Shampin, cracking a menacing smile.

Shampin rolled out a map. Mapmakers had been busy drawing plans of Amazonia. They were very basic as they had only been there for a few months but that had been long enough to make enough progress to help the soldiers read the basic lay of the land. Shampin pointed at an area of forest on the map that they had named Alpha section.

"You are to take your men to this forest tomorrow and clear it! We need a large supply of wood for the King's castle and to reinforce the perimeter fence. Further building of the soldier accommodation will continue once this has been completed. Cut all the trees down and then have them moved to this area here!" Said Shampin as he used his sword to point at an allocated space where hundreds of trees had already been cut down."Do you have any questions?"

"Are there any Amazonians living in this forest Sir?"

"I am not sure if there are or not. But if there are I am sure you can persuade them one way or another to leave" said Shampin.

"Yes sir!"

"You have one week, so work your men hard and reward will be with you all," continued Shampin as he turned his back signalling for Seltrecmore to leave.

He bowed his head and then left the tent.

Seltrecmore was a good man. He was a powerful soldier and a good leader but had never lost the quality of heart. He was not without sorrow for what the army and the King had done to the land and its people in Amazonia. He had great respect for his King as well, which made the feelings he experienced quite challenging to process. He made plans to carry out his orders, but at the same time he wished for a peaceful solution to the problem. As with all magic and requests of the heart, when Seltrecmore allowed this emotion to flow from him, unbeknown to him, a stream of light left his heart and fell into the earth.

The following morning section ten was called for a meeting, and its task was relayed. Everyone was happy to receive their orders, knowing that good food and drink would be their reward.

The demise of the balanced, happy environment of Amazonia continued, with one hundred men and one hundred axes all cutting down yet more trees. Animals started to run and leave their homes and some trees started to quiver in the space they were standing in. Every single one of them knew what was to occur and nothing could be done about it. Older trees looked to each other and smiled. They had happily shared their lives and would be together again in the sacred land where time does not exist. So they stood in silence as their brothers and sisters were cut, watching and listening to them crash and fall to the ground. What a mighty sound. There is a saying that asks if no one was is in a forest when a tree falls, does it make a sound. But today there were many in the forest, all listening to the cracking sounds of falling trees. The unseen magic of nature spirits and the loving inhabitants of the forest started running and flying all over the place as their homes were being demolished. Fairies were flying in all directions, and the little folk were running as fast as they could to move out of the way of the Mophead's feet and falling trees. Flowers, grasses, trees and roots all tried to stand their ground as change occurred around them.

After the first days work, the Mopheads marched back to their tents and left quite an eerie site behind them. The sun had started to set and vast areas of the forest had crashed to the floor, trunks and branches lay like broken bones on the ground. Most of the remaining trees, silhouetted in the pink sky were silent but some younger trees were crying and calling out for help. The little folk who were hiding at the edge of the forest came running as soon as the coast was clear of the axe-wielding Mopheads.

"It's ok!" came a little voice. It was Primrose, the fairy, hovering around a young tree who was crying.

"No it's not! My family have been cut and demolished around me, how is that ok?

They are also coming back in the morning! What would you have me do?" The tree asked in an angry but frightened way.

"Is there not a way you could find to walk away from here?" Primrose was full of concern for all of the trees.

"Do you not think my brothers and sisters would have done this if there was a chance to do so!"

"I don't know, I just think that we have lived in peace forever and have never even thought of anything other than how we live. But who is to say that trees cannot walk?"

The little tree smiled and tried to take a step. He made lots of noise, and his roots pulled at the earth that had nurtured him for so long - but nothing happened. The other younger trees tried to do the same, but they too were left standing strong within the earth.

Primrose started to shout out. "I know of a magic tree, and he is very wise! I bet he could tell you how to walk and I am sure he can help all of us because something needs to be done! If I could only find him in time, but I don't know where he lives! I will have to go and find my friends, they'll know. But I don't know if there is enough time to save you!" Primrose was now flying around in a frenzy as her energy was full of anguish.

"It's not just me, what about all the other hundreds of trees here, they say nothing, it is as though they have gone to sleep. They just stand there with their wisdom, content on moving on to a place where time does not exist! Why? I do not understand!" The little tree scrunched up his face and clenched his branch fists.

Primrose flew over to a large, older tree. She asked the question that the young tree had asked but he said nothing. Just then a female tree spoke.

"We have lived as a forest for thousands of years and nothing else we are. We love our life here, but at the same time we do not fear death and we do not fear change" she said, offering her wisdom to those who would listen.

"Well I do and I don't want to die! What about all you other young ones, do you agree with me?" Asked the little tree.

"Yes… yes, we do! Yes, we do too, so please, help save us as well as yourself!" came a flow of voices through the remaining forest.

The older trees just smiled and allowed the younger ones to live out their dreaming.

"I have an idea for now. I can make all of you invisible! That way, you have a chance to stay alive. All you need to do is to make sure that any trees around you that have chosen to do nothing, do not crash into you when they are cut, or that any Mopheads can feel you" said Primrose buzzing with excitement.

"Oh, only that then!"

"Well, it's the best I can do for now! I will go for help. I need to find Old Rook and Wise Owl, they will know what to do and where to find the wise tree! By the way, what is your name, little tree?"

"Well, up until now I have not had a name, but you calling me Little Tree is not very helpful with all that is to happen. I need a bigger name. I think you can call me Elma from now on. Elma means courage."

"Ok, Elma, well, it is a pleasure to meet you. My name is Primrose and I look forward to our epic journey ahead."

She then waved her fairy dust over all the trees that wanted to try and save themselves and said the following spell:

"Into the world of unseen dreams
All of you who are seen to be
In the here and now
Take a breath and disappear
And live for a while
Without a fear."

Once the words were spoken, everyone who wanted to, disappeared. Primrose laughed and zinged and was, for a moment, really happy with her magic. Then she remembered the task ahead of her. She called out goodbye to everyone, wished them good luck and flew off into the twilight.

The following morning section ten were back in the forest with their axes, and it was everyone for themselves. The devastation went on for days until the forest was clear, or so they thought!

A large number of young trees had managed to survive and were all very still within the earth of Amazonia. Elma had taken it upon himself to keep all the other young trees as calm as possible and felt that it was up to him now to save his brothers and sisters. So for now, they would invest their energies into faith and trust and believe that Primrose would return with help.

CHAPTER FIVE

The felled trees were dragged and cut and sliced and made ready to build the remaining sections of the King's castle. Once finished the Mopheads continued to take resources from the land to build houses and buildings for themselves.

Factories were created to make everything they needed, which then began to pollute the sky, air and water just like they had done to their homeland.

Water sprites accompanied by a large bird with a long neck, had gathered at a spot along the bank of the River Huma. They were most animated as they complained to each other about the condition of the river. Its beautiful crystal clear water had turned into a flow of toxic horror. It was yellow, brown and grey with foam that clung to the sides of the river bank. Before it had been polluted you could hear it sing along its way, as it carried with it the wisdom of the ages; the water that been there since the beginning of time.

"Don't shout at me! I did not make this mess, yes! I too want it all to go away, yes!

"But what am I to do?" Asked Silas the Strooner, a bird that looks a bit like a heron.

One of the water sprites sat on a rock and looked at Silas. "You know, that's the thing, you can't on your own as I can't on my own, but together, surely something can be done!" Said the Sprite.

A pixie approached with her hands on her hips and dressed in green dungarees that were far too big for her. "Yes, yes, that all sounds very heroic, but think about it, they have an army of Mopheads with axes and swords, and we have a load of Amazonians that are doing nothing with their long arms to bring about any peace or change to this situation!"

Silas moved towards the pixie waving his arms. "Ah, more negative rubbish from a pixie! You see how contagious negative thinking and being are and how quickly they engulf everything unless you are super aware all the time, which you, obviously, are not!"

"I am not negative, we were never negative. All I am saying is that we are not in a position to help ourselves here," shouted the pixie.

"You see!" said, Silas.

Through the edge of the forest, near to where they sat, emerged a unicorn who walked proudly yet gently towards them. It was an amazing sight!

"Where did you come from Light? We have not seen you in years! Enquired Silas.

"We were told that you had gone to another dimension!"

"I did, but sometimes I visit old friends. I am here because I received a message from the standing stones who live towards the West. I have been investigating ever since. The water sprite is right. There are many of you all calling for change, and one thing we can be sure of is change. So let's make it for the better!"

"What I want to know is how they got here!" said the pixie, standing on a rock with her hands still on her hips.

"That, my friend, is an excellent question," replied Light.

"Well, what is the answer?" Asked everyone in unison.

"It is a question that I will answer but not at this time," said Light, looking to all of them.

"What kind of answer is that!"

"Calm yourself pixie, I will explain everything. There is a gathering to happen very soon, and I will pass the information on to everyone at that point."

"What gathering, what are you talking about? You just make more confusion and speak more dibble dabble, how does that help?" Pushed the pixie again.

Silas glared at her. "Be quiet! I trust Light in his wisdom and so should you, if he says that he will answer the question and there is to be a gathering, then there will be. Light is a visionary and has a very high vibration, and you should trust his speak."

Light bowed his head. "Thank you, my friend." He turned to walk in the direction of the forest and then transformed into a beautiful iridescent light, just before he disappeared.

"Whoa-what happened there?" said Heather the bozy. Bozies look a little like your rabbits but they are much furrier.

"I told you all, did I not? Light is a high vibrational being that walks between realms and lives mostly on another dimension to ours."

"Oh, I see, well that explains a lot then, I think!" said Heather, pulling up her knees to her chest as she lay on her back laughing.

They gathered around and talked until the sun started to set on another day at which point they all went their separate ways but with hope in their hearts that things were about to get much better.

CHAPTER SIX

The Mopheads' time in Amazonia had led her to become like their former home, called Desirent. Amazonia had started to become sick. Rubbish was left all over the place, and no one would ever thank the land for all the food that it grew for them. This was so very different from the natural rhythm and mutual respect the Amazonians had with the land in the past.

Eventually, Amazonia became so dirty that the air was smelly and grey, the water went brown, and even the birds stopped singing. So many animals had decided to run away. They loved Amazonia so much and it broke their hearts to see her suffer but they wanted to go somewhere else to find peace. Thousands of trees had been cut, flowers trampled and killed. What a difference in such a short space of time.

This did not seem to bother the King and the Mopheads as they went on with their daily routine of destruction. But it did bother them when the land stopped producing food, and the water was no longer drinkable. The King was furious. He instructed the Mopheads to gather all the Amazonians and all his folk from Desirent so he could address them all.

One cold, grey morning, everyone collected to hear the King's address. He stood on a large platform in front of his nearly built castle. The wind was blowing, and his huge flag thrashed above him as his squeaky voice carried on the air.

"Your land was fine not so long ago, you must know how to fix this problem, and you will fix this problem. Otherwise, there will be trouble!"

The King turned around in a fury and walked into the castle leaving everyone bewildered, they had no idea what to do. Neither the wise Amazonians nor the dense Mopheads knew about the crystal caves or the dwarves that worked so hard to maintain them which contributed to the health of the land. They did not realise that the lack of love, happiness and respect for the environment had meant the crystals had stopped energising the land and were no longer helping in the production of their food and maintaining beautiful clear waterways.

Seigfreid was the wise elder responsible for all the dwarves. He was the overseer of all the work that had to be done in the caves as well as being counsel to those in his clan that had any problems. He was part of a long tradition where sons and daughters born to his family line were taught from an early age the wisdom of the caves. When one passed from this world to another, the next in line would take the role of wise leader and caretaker.

Dwarves had been the custodians of crystals and gems throughout the ages and Seigfreid understood so well about the energy of the beautiful crystal beings and the caves that they inhabited. The crystals beneath Amazonia like other crystal caves in other parts of the planet held the wisdom of the ages and had a frequency and vibrational energy field that helped the land and its fertility.

Seigfreid was a humble dwarf, but it was not for him to work so much with the physical chores of the caves. He was dressed well in comparison to the rest of the dwarf clan who laboured hard during their working day. He always wore a green checked jacket with pockets that had folds on the top, and dark brown trousers that came to just above his knees. But like the other dwarves, he would never consider wearing shoes or boots. Bare feet allowed the energy from the earth and the body of a dwarf to meld into each other.

The connection with the earth kept them balanced, nourished and connected to Amazonia and the planet of Mystery.

Seigfreid was aware that things were not right above him, as the crystal caves had stopped glowing. That evening, he took the long walk down to a special private chamber with a fire torch to light the way, as he wanted more insight as to what had occurred above him. Inside the chamber was a deep underground spring that would bubble up into a rock pool. Only the wise elder was allowed in here.

Seigfreid, as all the elders before him, was a seer. He could look into the water and see what was happening. He would focus on what he wanted to know, and the answer would be shown to him. Seigfreid walked along and quietly stood in front of the pool. His eyes grew large, and his frown deepened as he saw the destruction that had occurred above him. Holding his chin and chewing his lip, Seigfreid rolled his eyes around in his head. What was to be done?

He called a meeting of the clan and explained in his wise way what was happening. The response was one of anger, which he quickly calmed.

"This is not the way. I will seek counsel with Rook and Owl who live above us, and we will address this problem with love."

He stood there for a while and just emanated peace and calmness until everyone was calm and quiet again.

Seigfreid reassured everyone. "Now, all go back to your homes and share food and drink. I do not want you to worry. Instead, use your energy for the good, send love to the situation and picture everything being well."

Seigfreid then went on his way, and everyone else did as they were asked, and trusted that their wise leader would find a solution to the problem.

Seigfreid and the rest of the dwarves were not the only ones who wanted change. The Amazonians, animals and all the magical elementals, trees, flowers, the air and water were just a few of those living on the land that could not believe what was happening to their home. Eventually, they started to talk amongst themselves about how they might bring about change.

Seigfreid ate a meal with his wife Eleanor and explained what he was going to do. He was to leave the next morning to find Rook and Owl. They had been friends for years as their families had been connected throughout the ages.

"Would you like me to come with you?" Eleanor asked with a worried resonance in her voice.

Eleanor was a beautiful dwarf, with the softest of faces. Warm, rounded cheeks and beautiful blue eyes, with soft locks of hair falling to her shoulders. Seigfreid smiled at his wife. They had been married for nearly seventy years, and they loved each other very much.

Seigfried gave her a big hug and smiled into her soul. "It's ok Elley, I need you here."

Elley was also known for her wisdom and helped support the clan. But her role was that of a healer and midwife to the dwarf kingdom.

"Ok, Seigfreid, just be careful."

After climbing out of the underground caves and an evening walk, he arrived at old Owl's place, a beautiful ancient tree. The two of them were the best of friends and old Owl really was old and he was a little deaf but he saw Seigfreid coming a mile off. He flew to meet him and both were happy to have met again, even though the circumstances were not as they would like them. Owl heard of the troubles in the crystal caves and was concerned about how much the trouble had spread. They both agreed there was no time to waste and that they needed to find Rook.

"So where is Rook these days?" He asked old Owl.

"Well, he is a little everywhere. After his own tree was cut down by the Mopheads, his family flew way off to find a safe place to re-home. Now Rook travels between there and here, aware that something needs to be done about the Mopheads. We all have a feeling that something will happen, but as yet, up until you arriving, we have been unsure of how or when. But it clear now that whatever is to happen has started."

"Do you know where Rook is now?"

"Ummm, no, not really." Replied Owl with a puzzled look "The best thing to do is let me sit for a while and send out a telepathic message to him and see if he picks it up."

"That sounds like a plan. I can sit here, make a fire and put on a brew. Do you want some nettle tea, Owl?"

"No, no not really, but thank you for offering. You just do what you need to do, and I will try and connect with Rook."

Just then Rook flew in.

"Whoa, that was quick work!" Said Seigfreid.

"No, not really, I had not even started."

"Hey, Seigfreid, my friend, how are you? Oh my goodness you are here. It was on my mission plan to come and find you, but it has been so busy with everything that is going on," fluttered Rook.

"Yes, it does seem to be a big mess, but not to worry, I have a plan!"

"Ah, those words are like, well, I can't even think of anything right now that would describe what you have just said, except maybe honey rolling down my throat." laughed Rook.

They all started to laugh and then settled down to work on the plan. After hours of deliberation, it was decided that they would call a meeting. A note was written to explain where and when the meeting would take place and made it quite clear that everybody should attend. They also wrote in large writing for everyone to travel in silence to the meeting so as not to alert the Mopheads or the Amazonians of their plan. The note was then handed to a tree and once read they would pass the note from her branch to another tree. The trees would pass the message down to anyone whom they met along the letter chain and once someone read the message, they too would pass on the word and pass the message back up to the tree. Rook also instructed the birds, and they flew around as winged messengers. Within a few hours, everyone was aware of the meeting and gathered together two hours before sunset the following evening.

Everyone had walked gently and quietly from their homes to avoid the Amazonians, Mopheads and the King's soldiers. They were very intent to bring about change, although at the moment they had no idea how.

The noise level started to rise a little as they began to express their feelings of anger and despair about the situation in which they were living. Seigfreid asked a large Oakley tree to help bring everyone to quiet. He agreed and used his commanding presence to bring about hush.

"Ahem! Would you all please be quiet so wise Owl, Rook and Seigfreid can be heard as they would like to address you! Also, it would be wise not to raise the attention of the Mopheads, so being calm and balanced as you know how, would help in so many ways!"

He then used a few of his branches to stop some young pixies from running around and sat them down on a tree log that was covered in moss.

Rook thanked the tree and then proceeded to address the crowd.

"We are all aware of the changes and destruction to our land, and we all feel that something must be done and I have discussed this with Owl and Seigfreid.

Seigfreid from the crystal caves has an idea that may bring a solution to the problems of our environment."

Everyone started to talk amongst themselves and so the noise level began to rise again. Seigfreid raised his voice a little and continued.

"We will work our magic, but it requires the help of an Amazonian child whose heart is full of pure love and who has some ancient forgotten knowledge within his soul."

The crowd began to murmur again, and the level of unease began to rise. Just then, Primrose the fairy arrived.

"Thank goodness I have found you, Rook!" As she looked around, she saw that Owl and Seigreid were there as well. "How amazing that you are all here together, I could have only dreamt this! Truly amazing! I needed to find you all, and I have found you all in the same place! Magic is at work, thank goodness! I need help with the young trees!" buzzed Primrose.

"Primrose, calm yourself we are in the middle of a meeting," said Owl.

"But what I have to say is important too!"

"Maybe you would like to tell us all what you have to come to know," said Siegfried as he tried to calm her down.

Primrose went on to explain everything that she had experienced so far with the young trees and the destruction of their families. Everyone was sad to hear of her tale as it just impacted more upon all that they had experienced already. But Seigfreid assured them that their plan would work and all would be well.

"So Seigfreid, where do I find the very large magic tree called Chemini? I need to find him to get the magic wisdom of how to make the trees walk. I told them I would be back as soon as I could, so we need to be quick!"

"Ah, I can help you with that, but we also need to find this young child who can help with the much larger picture of what is happening as well."

"What young child and what bigger picture, Seigfreid? I need to find the tree!"

"I know of such a child who can help us, a boy," came a voice from the shadows in the forest.

Everyone turned to look in the direction of the voice and then a unison of "Aaahh" arose as Light the unicorn walked towards them in majestic beauty. His mane flowing like light-filled water with sparkling silver energy surrounding all of him.

"Hello, my dear friend! How have you been within your inter-dimensional travels?" Enquired Seigfreid.

Light smiled. "I know of the tree that Primrose asks of and I also know of the child you seek. My kind placed the higher light frequencies within this child's lineage and many other children's hearts. We chose one in every Kingdom just in case this moment ever arose. It was to ensure that extra help would be available when it was needed. And it was always believed that everyone working together for the good of their planet would help to resolve any problems.

"Well, why didn't you come and tell us this before!" shouted out a water nymph.

"I understand the place you speak from, but I am not responsible for how our journey unfolds. I AM but a part of it and it is now that I am here with the help," spoke Light in a very assured way.

Just then, Silas the Strooner moved forward and asked the question that he knew would be answered today. "We asked you before, how is it that these Mopheads got here in the first place?"

"Yes, yes," came from the crowd.

"We have all been thinking on this, no one knows where they came from, we have never seen or heard of the likes of the Mopheads in all of our history, so how is it they just arrived here?" Asked an old Spriklet screwing up his wrinkled face and rubbing his long nose.

"This question is going to be answered. But you all have to open your hearts and minds and let go of all that you believe for my answer to be heard. You all see me as a multidimensional being now, and because of the situation at hand, in some way, you have just accepted this fact. This is a good thing, but just comprehend for a moment what I have said and realise how much of the unknown you have just accepted. Now, let us go a little further. Quite a way from here to the West is a place where no one really visits because of the distance and the terrain. Hidden within a forest clearing next to a wild meadow is a stone circle. It is a portal to other worlds." The unicorn cleared his throat and took another deep breath.

Light was very aware that what he was saying was a lot for everyone to take in and to believe, but he had to keep them onside with what he was saying, and he did not have much time to do it in.

"A long, long time ago, there were some elders who lived amongst you but would not show their true identity. They were here as custodians to you and your land. They would travel through the star-gate generated at the stone circle to other lands just like yours, making sure all was well. At one point in history, a battle started and the beings who were not of the light were intent on coming to many planets including Amazonia to claim it for themselves. It was then decided to place a force field around the stone circle which would close the multidimensional portal or star-gate as it is known, to everyone including the less than light beings who wanted to attack. Before the elders left Amazonia, they placed knowledge within the heart of a child, which was then passed down to their children's children, but it was held in a way that would only be released in such times as now." Light took another breath.

The silence all around was deafening, no one moved or spoke, and most mouths were wide open and everyone's eyes were transfixed on Light.

"That is crazy!" Said a voice.

Seigfreid appeared next to the water nymph who had just spoken and stared right into his eyes and heart and asked for him to find the truth within and to follow his passion to help bring peace to the land.The nymph looked backed at Seigfreid and found peace and smiled as he agreed to work with the rest of the group. He was not sure what had just happened to him but did not wish to dispute or disagree with any of the plan anymore.

"But if there was a force field around the portal, why is it that the Mopheads have managed to get through?" Asked Heather the Bozie.

"King Atman's grandfather, who is now in spirit, worked with the less than light at great lengths to help his grandchild and his people leave their home in search of a new place to live, but we have no more information than that. What I can tell you, is that an intergalactic council has taken on board all my concerns and have interceded to place a new forcefield around the circle with an impenetrable coding that is now the sole responsibility of the Council.

Everyone was so amazed by what they heard, the night was full of magic, from inter-dimensional unicorns, to portals and intergalactic councils, how could their plan fail!

"So where do we find the tree?" Said Primrose as she popped up again, not at all surprised by what had just been spoken. She lived a life of magic every day, and none of it fazed her at all. "I so need to help the trees escape the forest before anything else is done!" Primrose flew right up in front of Seigreid's face looking up into his left eye.

Light walked up to Primrose and agreed to help her and asked for everyone to be quiet. Light himself also went very quiet, and the energy around him turned into a rainbow-coloured aura. Next, the tip of his single golden horn extended into the most exquisite vortex, spinning way up into the sky and beyond. Everyone was in awe but was soon shocked out of that state by the unicorn moving into the vortex and disappearing.

"Where has he gone? Did he not just hear me ask for help? Did he not just agree to help me and the trees? Did he just disappear!"

"Yes, where has he gone?" shouted the crowd.

"Shhhhh!" hushed Seigfreid. "You have to keep quiet, we know the Mopheads and Amazonians are around, how many times must I ask you to be quiet!"

Next, there was an image in the sky. It was like watching a moving picture as the unicorn talked to a large tree.

"Hello, Chemini!" said Light to the tree.

"Hello, my dear friend. It has been such a long time. I knew you would come, you had to. There is so much to put right. I am living with trust that this is all for a reason and all will be well, but it is very testing!" Chemini continued to pour his heart out to Light.

"It will all work out Chemini, it always does. It's just sometimes, things seem to be worse than others, when in reality it is all the same."

Chemini smiled. "So what do we need to do?"

"Firstly my friend, Primrose the fairy, is involved with helping some young trees. She is trying to prevent them from being felled as they have decided to live through these changes that are occurring in the forest. She has turned them invisible for now, but somehow knows that you have magic to help the trees walk free!"

"Yes, I do! They are brave youngsters and will take leadership amongst the rest of the forests as they grow older and wiser. Ask of them to say the following chant:

Forever I am a tree
Forever I am a tree
The sun shines
The light rains
Together we will be free.

Then primrose will have to take some magic water and place a few drops at the roots of each one who wishes to walk. You will find the water inside the hole in my body. A Silver Woodpiper made the hole so long ago, and the water has been kept clean and pure by the worker Silverlytes."

Light then used his mind's eye to call the water into his single golden horn.

The whole group was still watching the encounter between Chemini and Light from the meeting place, and all they kept saying was "aaaaaaah!" It was truly amazing, and they all felt so blessed to be part of what was happening before their very eyes.

"So what else do you require from me?" Asked Chemini to Light.

"Ah, I am to bring you a boy, an Amazonian boy with sacred energy within his heart that will work with you to bring about change. I will tell you more when we next meet."

Light thanked Chemini the tree and then again used his mind's eye to extend the energy vortex from his single horn and disappeared from the picture in the sky back to the meeting from where he had first left. As he arrived back, the image in the sky closed and everyone moved to be closer to him.

"So Primrose, do you have a flask to put this magical water in?" Asked Light.

"I can conjure one up!" As she spun around in the air very fast, golden dust encircled her and then on the ground in front of Light appeared a violet glass bottle.

"Ah, well done! Thank you; It is beautiful."

Light moved the magical water from his horn into the bottle and Primrose listened to the words she was to say and commanded her self to remember them well.

"Primrose, go now to your trees and help them in your special way. Bring them back here with you, but ask for them to walk lightly! Tell them to stay away from where the Mopheads are working and ensure they are covered with enough dust to guarantee their invisibility."

Seigfreid then addressed the crowd. "My dear friends, Primrose will help the trees, and we will go and find the boy. We ask of you to keep faith and love in your hearts and trust all is well."

Everyone was so happy that there was a plan and they all went off to their homes trusting that all the magic they had witnessed would surely be able to help them and their land.

CHAPTER SEVEN

"I am here!" called Primrose to the trees.

Elma smiled and breathed a sigh of relief. "Ah, I knew you would come. Some of the others were losing faith, but I trusted you would be back with us. We are very fortunate, the invisibility dust eventually wore off, but the soldiers had already left! Did you find who you were looking for? Have you brought us some help?"

"Indeed I have! First of all, I am going to say some magic words, then I am going to put three drops of magic water from this bottle to the roots of all those who wish to walk free. Once everyone is ready, I will then turn you all invisible again except for one leaf on each each of you so we can all see where everyone is!"

"That sounds like a good plan."

"Yes it is, but there is much to do. The whole of Amazonia is in trouble, and we are all going to help!"

Elma shrugged up his branches. "And how do you suppose we are going to do that?"

"I will explain as we make our way, but first we have to get all of you walking, so let's get on with it! You will all have to say these magic words."

Primrose spoke the words out loud, and all the trees started to repeat them after her. They said it over and over again as she flew around with the magic violet bottle that never seemed to run dry. Every time she came to a tree who wished to walk free, Primrose would place three drops on to its roots. She then instructed them to keep repeating the magic chant together.

"Forever I am a tree
Forever I am a tree
The sun shines
The light rains
Together we will be free."

Primrose zinged with excitement. "Ok! I am not sure how this works, really, but let's all try to walk."

Each one of the trees used its heart and soul to focus on the act of walking, and it was then that the earth opened around them and their roots were exposed, and they began to move.

"Oh my goodness, it worked!" Screamed Primrose.

"We have a problem! We can move, but we cannot balance, we only have one leg! What are we to do?" Called Elma.

Primrose thought hard for a quick second. "I have a great idea. Everybody take a partner, the tree to your right or left and hold arms! Each one of your trunks is a leg, so you can lean against each other to balance and then you can walk!"

Primrose was tickled pink with her idea, so much so she started to glow pink. Elma just looked on at her and rolled his eyes around as it was only one more thing to have to digest in this ever-changing world around him. Each tree decided to trust in Primrose and followed her instructions, so much so that her plan worked and they began to walk with balance.

"Oh, hold on, we need to turn you all invisible, there is nothing like a bunch of large trees walking across the landscape to let the Mopheads and Amazonians know something is happening... right!" Buzzed Primrose.

She waved her magic dust and again all were invisible except one leaf on each tree. Fifty trees in total were now to walk with Primrose to meet up with Seigfried and his friends. They were to follow the river and to stay as far away from the villages as possible, each keeping an eye and ear out for any signs of Amazonians and especially the Mopheads and the King's soldiers.

"This is amazing, I feel so different! I mean, I don't feel any less tree-like but walking and moving as a team makes me feel like I can go anywhere! My Mother always told me that I could go anywhere with my mind, but I never quite got what she meant. So this, this is amazing, and this works!" said Elma.

"Can I do this forever?" Asked another tree.

"I am not sure, can we just take one thing at a time; first, we have to save Amazonia," Primrose said, holding up her arm that was oozing fairy strength. "We can work out how you are going continue expressing yourself as a tree after we have solved a few more problems."

A tree smiled, stretching the bark around his mouth, making the lines around his eyes lift. The contagious energy of lightness started to make everyone smile and laugh, which was a good thing. There had been too much sadness and fear for far too long.

"Ok, let's go!" Said one of the young trees.

"I am just getting the hang of walking - Woah - this is really strange, I feel like my sides are going stretch me in half as I move! How long has it been since trees walked, nearly one hundred years, maybe a thousand years?" Asked another tree.

"You just have to get your balance and start talking to your roots as an extension of yourself to walk instead of stand," replied Primrose, not quite knowing how she knew what she had just said.

"So how am I meant to get food and water if I not connected into the earth?" Asked another tree.

"Good question, when we rest just nestle your roots into the earth, and you can get all your needs but remember you get much of what you need through the sun!" Primrose was exuberant with her new knowledge.

"How do you all know all of this Primrose?" Asked Elma.

"I am not sure. I have a feeling the presence of Light the unicorn is with me."

"Light the unicorn, who is that?"

"Oh, yes, another story, but trust me, he is a wonderful, magical being who has your best intentions at heart."

"I trust you, Primrose, that is all that matters right now."

"Ah Elma, that is so sweet!" And she flew up to his face and gave him a magical kiss on his nose.

Elma smiled, and Primrose giggled away.

Primrose flew up into the air so she was at eye level with most of the trees. "Ok everyone, the time has come, let's go and let's go quietly!"

The sun was setting as they made their way down to the river holding arms and following Primrose.

"Ooooh, paddling!" Said a tree as she placed her root feet into the water and started to laugh."It feels like liquid light moving between the very fibres of my being. Why have we not walked before? All trees should be liberated from the shackles of the earth," she said.

"Earthing does not shackle you," said her walking partner."We are all here to play our part, and our part is so important! If we all just got up and walked around all day, who would hold the substance of Mystery together? When it rains, she would wash away! And what about all the animals that love to live by us or within us? What about the birds that fly around but always come back home?"

"Oh, yes of course! I was so busy thinking about all of this, I forget the essence of what it means to be a tree. I still think we should be allowed to move around at least for a few hours. I think when we find this magic tree, Chemini this is something I want to ask for all of us."

"Come on. We have to meet with Seigfreid who is on a mission to save Amazonia. Primrose said, busily spinning around like a sparkler.

"What do you mean?" The trees called out to her.

"Ah, I will tell you all about Seigfreid and the magic underworld kingdom as we travel. Now please, come on!"

It was very late in the day when the trees and Primrose approached the place where Seigfreid had agreed to meet them all. It was all very quiet, and there were not many stars shining through as all the pollution had started to keep the night sky very murky. The trees crept along, keeping their wits about them. Making progress was challenging now, as in this light it was more or less impossible to see the one leaf they had left exposed, and so the trees started to bump into one another.

"Hey, be careful!" Said a tree.

"Ooh, so sorry, it is a little tricky now to see."

"It's ok. Said Primrose. "We are here now, I can see Seigfreid, Rook and Owl! Just all stand still and make yourselves comfortable. Place your roots into the earth so you feel steady, and that will help you relax and then you can have a snooze."

"Welcome my dear. You have indeed succeeded in such a great endeavour. We are grateful for your courage and fairy powers!" Said Seigfreid to Primrose.

"Ah Seigfreid, it was nothing! I actually had a lot of fun! Come and meet the trees!"

Siegfried walked down towards the trees with Rook and Owl flying by his side.

"Welcome my friends," said Owl, to the trees.

"Yes, welcome! I am so very sorry for the loss of your brothers and sisters and the destruction of your home. I trust the plan we have will help restore order and peace to our land," said Seigfreid.

"Thank you so much, Seigfreid. Primrose has told me so much about all of you and that you have a plan. We are very grateful for all that you are, and if we can offer our service in any way we are more than happy to help," smiled Elma, who was feeling very proud of himself for being part of rescuing his forest friends.

"That is so kind of you, but for now we need to go on a little mission of our own. We want you to stay here and rest and recover from your long journey."

Primrose flew up to Elma and his friends. "I will now place more dust around you, so there is no way it will wear off before I return. You will be safe here. There is no reason for anyone to walk down this far to where we are, so do not worry about anyone or anything bumping into your invisible selves."

"We are so grateful to you Primrose, who could say what would have happened to us if it were not for your courage and inspiration. We are forever in your debt and we will always call you our friend."

As everyone quietly went on their way, the trees nestled their roots into the earth, closed their eyes and started to relax into a deep, deep sleep.

CHAPTER EIGHT

Seigfreid, Rook and Primrose walked down to the river stepping over moss-covered rocks and holding on to stunted ancient woodland to catch their footing over the rocky terrain which, so far, was untouched by the Mopheads. The air was wet and cold, and Seigfreid lit the way with a lantern that had a cap over the top to stop the light beaming upwards, so their presence would be less noticeable to any Mopheads or Amazonians in the area.

"Tell us about the boy, Seigreid. Who is he? Where does he live and why him?" Said Primrose, frantically flying around Seigfreid's head.

"So many questions for such a small being!" Laughed Siegfried with his face lighting up in its magical way. Even in the low light his sparkling eyes and smile were still as bright as in the day.

"The boy's name is Sam. He is the son of a healer called Rachel. His family ancestors were given the gift that Light has spoken of and Sam is now the holder of that gift."

"How do you know that, and how do you know where he lives?" Enquired Primrose.

"Ms Primrose, I am a seer, yes? I also have a magical pool within the caves where I live that no one until now has heard of except the lineage of myself. But times are changing, and more of our magic is being revealed. You saw Light earlier on. He showed much to all of those who were watching, and I too know now, there is much to share with everyone."

"Ooh, more magic please Seigfreid, you know me, magic, magic, magic!" She laughed.

The group continued to walk in search of Sam. Finally they reached the bottom of the valley where the river was travelling very fast and sounded disheartened and angry. Seigfreid led them alongside the river in the opposite direction to which she flowed, and after about ten minutes they arrived at a small house built around a big old tree. All the lights were off but the last embers of the fire left its warm glow around Sam's room.

"We are here!" Whispered Siegfreid.

"How do we get in?" Asked Rook.

"If you open a window, I could fly inside and try to open the door. I am not sure how much trouble the door will be, but I can give it a go."

"No need, Rook. But thank you for offering. I am calling on the magic of the ancients as they are supporting us in our important mission. They will help me open the door, just wait and see!"

Just then the door opened all by itself. Everybody smiled to each other and felt the love and support all around them.

Once inside Sam's house, they quietly looked for his bedroom where they found him fast asleep. It was a warm and cosy space with room for the three of them to stand around his bed. They gently woke Sam up and as he opened his eyes he was instantly wide awake with the shock of all of them standing around him. Rook and Owl flew up and stood at the foot of his bed. But it only took a short while to feel really comfortable with the situation as they started toexplain what was happening to Amazonia. They spoke to him about the Mopheads and the environmental problems and how they needed his help to restore balance with the additional support from a wise tree as well as a lot of magic and love.

Chemini the magic tree was very old. No one knew his age exactly, but Seigfreid had read of Chemini in many journals written by his fore-bearers. They wrote about how much wisdom and magic was bestowed to the tree and how he could provide counsel in times of great need.

Sam was still amazed at Seigried and the talking birds. He had never met anyone like them. He had always believed in magic but had not experienced it and would only talk about it with his Mother.

"Yes, of course, I will help you. When do we start?"

"Now!" Said Rook.

"Come on, no more time to waste, let's go!" said Seigfreid.

Sam pulled on his trousers, put on his coat, hat and boots and called his dog Kit to come with him. Belle, the cat who was sleeping at the foot of Sam's bed just yawned. Magic was of no surprise to her, and she was miles too sleepy to be bothered by anything.

They quietly left the house so as not to wake Sam's mum and walked along the river path towards Chemini. Seigfreid carried his lantern to light the way with Sam and Kit by his side, while Primrose flew around them creating more light from her visible glowing auric field. Old Rook and Owl would fly from tree to tree, taking a rest each time they landed waiting for the others to catch up. They all continued along the path until finally they reached the place where Chemini stood. Old Rook flew up on to one of Chemini's branches and asked if he would talk to the group that had collected around his huge sprawling roots. Sam was amazed as the tree opened his eyes and began to speak.

"I have been expecting you," he said in a very old wise way.

"You have?" Asked Sam.

"Indeed I have. Light came to me and explained what was to be done. All the creatures and dwarfs and elementals know, it must just be you that is not up to speed with it all," he laughed.

Although he was laughing now, he had been unhappy and unsure about life because of all the destruction happening around him. But now he was slightly happier as he was surrounded by his friends and knew something was going to change for the better. He, like everyone else trusted Light the unicorn and was ready to do the work.

Sam was to hug, Chemini every night for two weeks sending him enormous amounts of love, while Seigfreid spoke magic words and burnt sacred herbs near to where Chemini stood. They asked Sam to begin although all the other ingredients of the ritual had yet to be organised. As Sam hugged the tree, Chemini was briefly filled with beautiful white light which then flowed down his roots into the earth and then stopped. All the dwarfs down in the earth caves jumped up with surprise and joy when they saw what was happening. The light was not that strong but was enough for them to see that something was indeed happening and they relayed this information to Seigfreid telepathically.

"This is good, Sam. The plan will work, all we need now is time and dedication to making our dreams and wishes of healing our land to come true," said Seigfreid.

"Well, how did that boy manage such a great feat. He is so young, and you did not even speak your words or burn your herbs!" Asked Chemini.

"Sam's whole lineage had a secret implant of coded information put into them a long, long time ago. When turned on, it has a huge power to do just what he was doing then and is far more powerful than he first appears!"

There was also a lot more to Sam than Chemini realised. Sam was also the son to Rachel, and that in itself was a significant advantage in his growing up. She was a healer of all folk. It made no difference to her who or what required healing. If anyone came to her door with their problems, she would do her best to help. Rachel exchanged her gift for whatever was being offered. Some would bring food, some would bring tokens, some would bring things that they had made or provided services. At one time Rachel and Sam had their roof mended in exchange for healing a whole family of Amazonians. Rachel had the magic in her heart to put her hands on the sick to make them better and Sam would sometimes sit and watch. He could see the light emitting from her hands as she placed them on whomever she was helping. Usually, the folk asking for help would feel the love and warmth from her heart and hands, but they could not see the light as Sam could. Rachel also loved nature as much as all the Amazonians did. But she went further with the connection, talking to everything as her brothers or sisters and encouraged Sam to do the same. This meant that Sam grew up in a home where magic was thought of as only love and it was lived as if it were the most natural way of being. Sam loved crystals too, and when the travelling sales-folk passed through Amazonia, he would take his saved tokens and buy a crystal every cycle. He also loved to make wands and would carve them out of sacred tree branches that had fallen with the wind and then bind some crystals or stones from the river on to them.

Sam looked up at Chemini and said, "I am delighted and honoured to be working with you for the greater good."

Chemini pulled a face to himself and relaxed his branches as he breathed out. Everyone thanked Chemini and wished him good dreaming, and then started their walk back to Sam's home. Standing outside his front door, Sam hugged his new friends and thanked them for the opportunity to help them. He expressed how happy he was to be exploring more of the magic that surrounded him and was so excited to be allowed to see the elemental folk as he knew this was a great honour and gift. When Sam went inside, he wanted to go and tell his mother all about what had happened. But he was asked not to share this information with Rachel until they had all finished their work. He had wanted to ask why but also understood that sometimes the question of why does not always have a simple answer. He hung up his coat and placed his boots carefully so he wouldn't alert his mum in the morning to any of his night-time adventure and quietly went back to bed.

The next morning Sam was woken up by Rachel. She fully opened the curtains and let the sunshine through. Sam just smiled.

"You look happy, Sam. Did you dream your dreams?"

"Yes I did, it was a great night for dreaming!"

"I am sure it was," said Rachel with a knowing look. "Well write it down, you never know what you may learn from it."

Sam smiled again. She was saying one thing, and he was saying another, but between them, there was an unspoken understanding.

"It's nearly time for you to go to forest school. Go and take your shower, brush your teeth, put on your clothes and then come and get your breakfast.

At forest school, Sam was itching to tell his friends Zallum and Angey all about his night-time adventure, but again he had to zip up his mouth and get on with his day.

"You look really happy today," said Zallum.

"Really? No more than usual. Maybe it's because the sun is out and there is magic in the air."

"What is it with you and magic?" he teased.

"Hey magic does exist, kind of..." said Angey rolling her eyes to the sky.

On that note, they all ran off down to the river with the rest of the forest school group to start building a den, something they all loved to do. At the end of the day, Rachel, as usual, was waiting for Sam, ready to walk him home.

Rachel greeted Sam with a big hug. "How was your day?"

"It was magic thank you." He had the same smile on his face from when he had first woken up.

Their walk home was the same walk that they had taken for years, but it was not as happy as it used to be. Soldiers walked around in their armour just to keep their presence known. They also had the Mophead village folk to contend with. They were quite a rude bunch who had no intentions of getting to know the Amazonians for who they really were. The forest school was allowed to be kept open as the King wanted to keep track of where the children were during the day and would send Mophead soldiers to survey the schools to see if any children showed promise in becoming new warriors for his army. Rachel was not concerned by this idea. She too had some kind of knowing within her that things would change for the better and trusted that Sam and the rest of the children would grow to adulthood in peace.

That evening Sam was so excited about what was to come later, he had to make up an excuse of how tired he was so he could go to bed early in preparation for another night- time adventure. Sam gestured a really long yawn as he stretched out.

"Ah Mum, I really am tired."

"Are you feeling ok, Sam-Sam?"

"Yep, I think so, just need to sleep."

Rachel dropped her head to the side and looked at him with a smile. She knew something was afoot but trusted Sam as she trusted herself and said that he had better go to bed. That night was the first night of the two-week plan. Every night for two weeks, he would creep out of his house with his new friends and walk along the river path to meet and hug, Chemini. Seigfreid would bring his sacred herbs to burn around the base of the tree, and while Sam was hugging Chemini, he would walk around the tree in a clockwise direction saying the magic words.

"For all the folk within one stroke
Let it be free for all of thee.
Take this spark of heartfelt herb
And let it be felt in the underworld hearth.
Let the love and flame shine through
Let thee be free
So let it be
We send you love and light
And wish for thee all to be free.
May the love of all that is
heal all
Through all that is."

Sam jumped down from Chemini, one branch at a time. Seigfried smiled, Rook nodded his head, Owl smiled on and Primrose was just ecstatic.

"So very good. So very, very good," said Owl.

Sam smiled as Chemini used a branch to hold him by the shoulder.

"I will see you all tomorrow then?"

Chemini so enjoyed the company of everyone visiting with him every night. The feeling of love was beautiful and Sam too was full of love for all his new friends. It was the first time that he had actually seen and heard a tree speak and was full more than ever with the magical wonder of his homeland.

Finally, on the fourteenth night, Chemini started to shake and glow, and the whole of the underground crystal caves gleamed and shone like silvery stars. Beautiful light and energy was then sent up into the Amazonian's land and beyond to all of Mystery. All the fruit and crops started to grow in an instant. In minutes the trees were full of fat ripe fruit, and the crops were ready for harvesting. The rivers and streams were gleaming and clean again with the fish and water life jumping and swimming with joy. The air began to clear and cleanse, and the birds found their voices and began to tune their environment. It was a truly magical, amazing, transformational feat.

CHAPTER NINE

When the Amazonians and Mopheads woke up in the morning, they found all their vegetable gardens were full of food and the trees were heavy with beautiful ripe fruit ready for picking. Everyone looked on and could hardly believe their eyes and then they all started to smile, laugh, sing and dance.

Seltrecmore went to the castle to inform the King of the transformation that had occurred to the land overnight. He explained how everyone was singing and dancing. The king jumped up from his large thrown, twirling around in a temper. He made his way outside to overlook the land and his people with the intention to stop all of the joy that apparently was in the air. However, he too was amazed at the changes on the land and in the air and in awe of the beautiful sight. Blue skies, sweet breezes, and the river was sparkling with so many diamonds that he could see it from the castle. He also noticed the abundant fruit and mesmerising flowers, and so he too started to smile and laugh and could not help but dance and what a dance it was. He even managed to jump and dance in his long green pointy shoes, and his cloak just flew around as he spun. His family came out to see what was happening and could not believe their eyes, and within minutes they too were laughing, dancing and hugging one another.

Sam and Kit walked through the village, and Sam stood on a tree stump and spoke very loudly. "Our land was dying! The reason our crops failed, and our fruits never came, why the water was sick and the birds stopped singing, and the skies were dull with pollution was because of the lack of love and respect for the land and one another. All of this created a darkness in the earth. It has been removed, but you must now live with happy hearts and agree to look after yourselves and the land with love and respect."

I hear what you say, boy! I can indeed understand now how my choices and lack of respect for the earth and all that dwell upon it have created a life that none of us can or should live. I hereby make my first promise in a new dawn that I will love and care for everyone and everything and expect everyone else to do the same. I believe this is a wholesome order, so let it be done!" Said the King as he danced and laughed.

The crowd cheered, and everyone turned to one another to hug and smile. Sam began to raise his voice so he could be heard above the cheering crowd.

"There is something else! You are all oblivious to the other beings that live amongst you. We have a magical community of elves, fairies, water nymphs and dwarves and so many more magical beings than you can possibly imagine living around us all the time. Their vibration is much higher than yours making it very difficult for you to see them. But I can assure you that they do indeed exist. It is because of them and the wildlife and nature all working together with love that we are given another chance to thrive. We also give thanks to King Atmat for being brave enough in seeing the error of his ways!"

At that moment Seigfreid made his appearance with Rook and Owl. They presented Sam with a pointy blue hat and thanked him so much for helping to save them and the land and told him that the hat was special and would keep him connected to all the magic within and around him. Seigfreid then addressed the crowd who were silent with shock but were also very excited about his presence.

"We the magical kingdom have agreed that the dwarfs, fairies, pixies, elves, gnomes and sprites and all the other magical beings will let you see us on special occasions! We trust that our sharing with you will be a reminder of the beauty and magic that surrounds you all day every day. As well, we ask you to remember that the animal kingdom needs to be loved and respected as if they were your own kind! You see, even the trees, rivers, flowers, in fact, all of nature are all part of you, as we are all one. Respect yourself, everyone and everything and we will all be well! I also want to give special thanks to a very old wise tree called Chemini and Light the Unicorn who helped us save Amazonia. I send love, light, peace and healing to you and all that you do!"

As Sam looked beyond the crowd he was filled with yet more joy and warmth as he saw his Mother standing next to Light. She was so very proud of Sam and all that he had been a part of. Sam new at that moment Light was the magical being that they were due to meet on the day when a loud sound had made them return home. He also realised that the loud sound that they had heard was the star-gate opening and the arrival of the soldiers. What a journey they had all been on.

Standing behind Light and Rachel were the walking trees which had nestled their roots into the ground. They were so happy to hear King Atmat, speak of respecting everyone and everything and felt safe, trusting that their lives would return to peace, even though some may go walkabouts every now and again!

Primrose zinged everywhere. What an adventure she had been on. Suddenly she felt, what was next, as life from this point on was never going to be the same again.

That night they did what the magical kingdom did best. They held a huge party for everyone to celebrate all the good that had been created. From that moment on everybody looked after everyone and everything, never wanting to return to the dark-times, but more than anything they all enjoyed the light.

The End.

ABOUT THE AUTHOR

Rachel Bolton, born in London in 1969 is a writer, artist, spiritual teacher, a student of astrology and a psychic channel for healing energy. She heals people and animals and has over twenty of years experience. You can read more about her work at www. rachelbolton.life. She has a passion for hand-sculpting clay and embodies her sculptures with healing energy that can be felt by others when they are near to them. Many of her sculptures manifest as unique elementals that have a life of their own. Rachel has a deep love for Mother Earth and all of her nature. Rachel lives at the foot of Dartmoor and spends hours walking her dog, Kit up on the Moor, in the woods, and by the rivers. She is a Mother to Sam who at the time of publishing this book turned seventeen years of age. Sam's education has spanned mainstream school, forest school, home education as well as a progressive democratic school. Rachel has written this book so it can be a voice for the world of elementals and all of nature. She dreams for everyone to love Mother Earth, themselves, each other and all of our animal and mammal friends.

To contact Rachel Bolton: www.rachelbolton.life